POM POM
gets the grumps

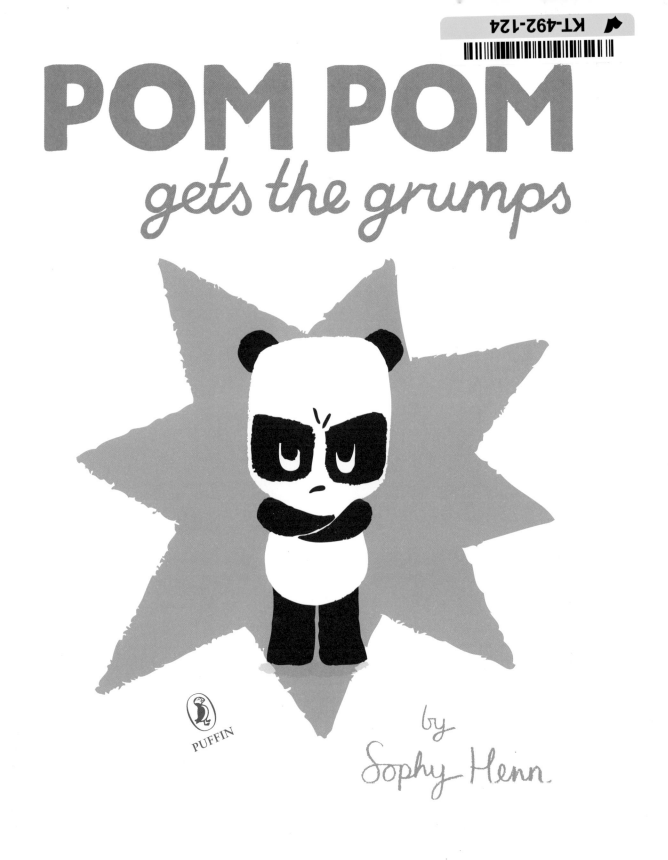

PUFFIN

by
Sophy Henn

One morning Pom Pom got out of bed
on the **wrong** side.

And then **nothing** was right.

His blanky, Timmington, couldn't be found.

Anywhere.

"Harrumph!" said Pom Pom.

His baby brother, Boo Boo,
        was playing with his favourite toy.

His cereal was soggy and
there were bits in his juice.

"Harrumph!" said Pom Pom.

Then things went from bad to worse . . .

His toothbrush was
too scratchy.

His flannel was just
freeeeeezing.

And he couldn't do
a thing with his hair.

"Harrumph!"
said Pom Pom.

After **all** that,
it was time to go.

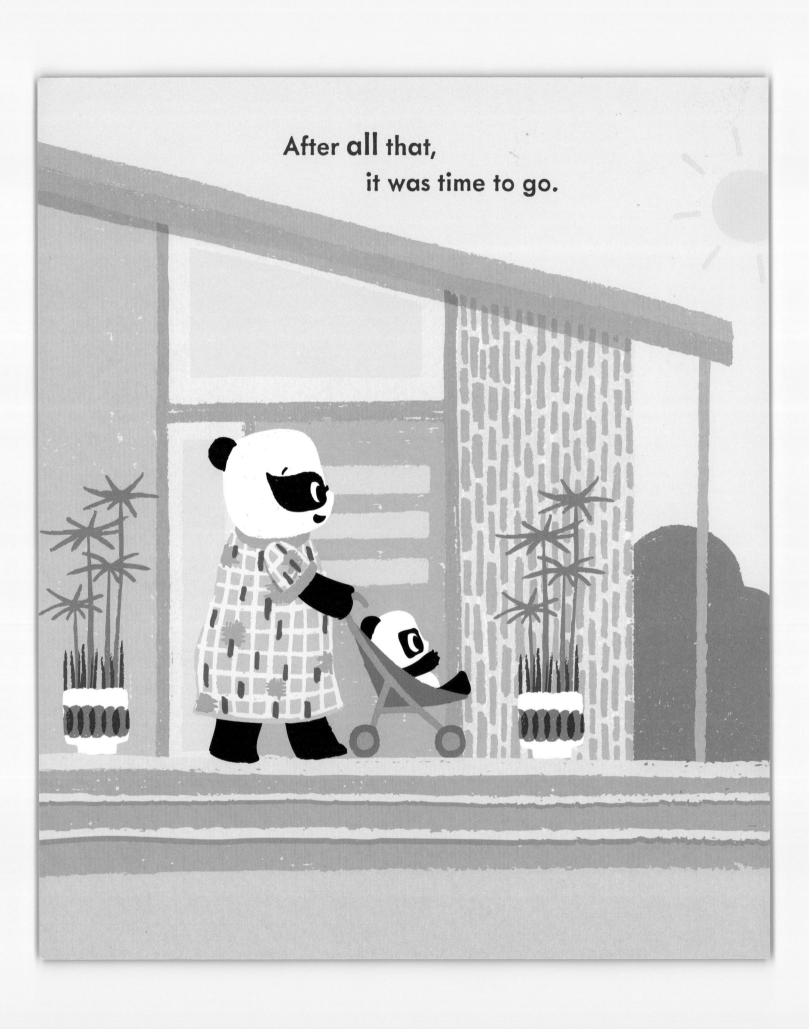

Outside the sun was too sunny.

And the birds
were too noisy.

"Harrumph!"
said Pom Pom.

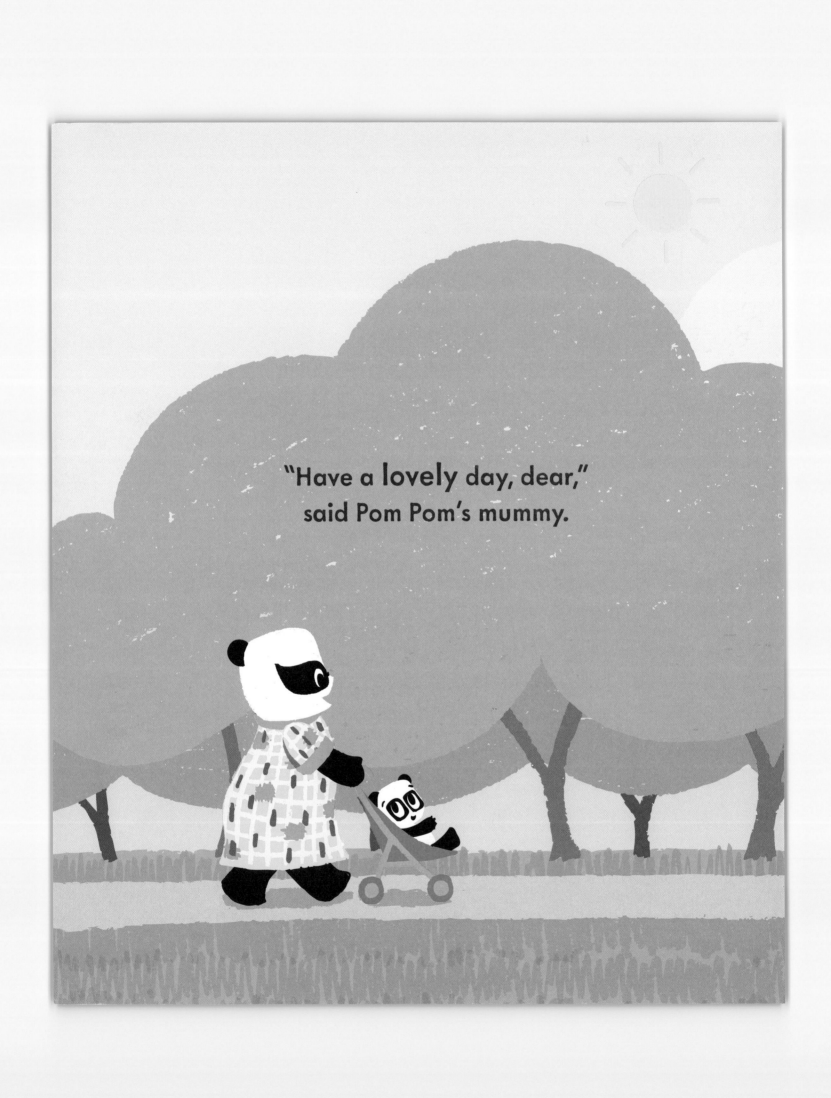

"Have a **lovely** day, dear,"
said Pom Pom's mummy.

"Harrumph!"
said Pom Pom.

In the playground everyone was having fun

8 9 10 11 12

Except
Pom Pom.

"Fancy a kickabout?"
asked Buddy.

"NO."
huffed Pom Pom.

"Want to watch ants?"
asked Rocco.

"NO."
grumbled Pom Pom.

"Would you like to play catch?"
asked Baxter.

"NO!"
shouted Pom Pom.

"Do you want to do skipping?"
asked Scout.

"G
AW

O
AY!"

yelled
Pom Pom.

And they did.

"oh."

Pom Pom didn't feel like shouting any more.
He felt sad. And a bit silly.
His friends had only tried to be nice.

"Oops,"
said Pom Pom.

And off he went to find the others.

"Sorry, everyone," said Pom Pom.

"That's OK,"
said everyone.

"I k

"L

11 12

"I'll be chaser," said Buddy.

"Yay!" said everyone.

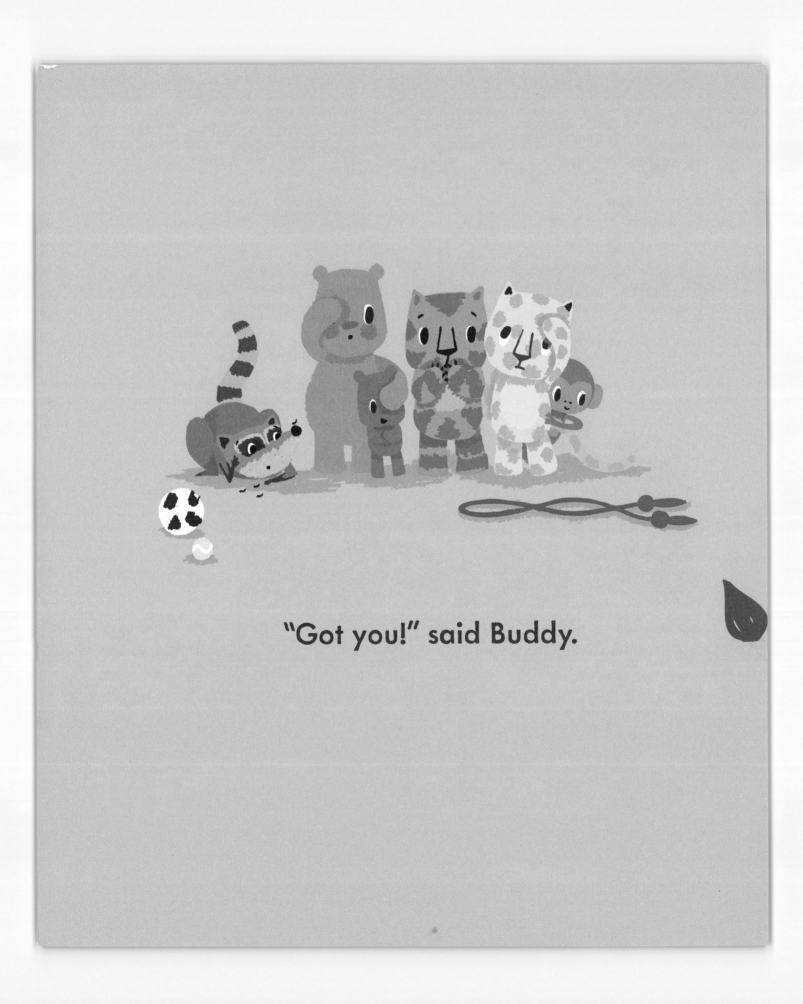

"Got you!" said Buddy.

"Harrumph!"
said Pom Pom.

For Rob

Who almost never gets the grumps!

x

PUFFIN BOOKS

UK | USA | Canada | Ireland | Australia | India | New Zealand | South Africa

Puffin Books is part of the Penguin Random House group of companies
whose addresses can be found at global.penguinrandomhouse.com.

www.penguin.co.uk   www.puffin.co.uk   www.ladybird.co.uk

First published 2015
This edition published 2016

001

Text and illustrations copyright © Sophy Henn, 2015
Made and printed in China
ISBN: 978–0–141–37094–1